I'LL FIX ANTHONY

BY JUDITH VIORST
PICTURES BY ARNOLD LOBEL

 Atheneum Books for Young Readers
New York London Toronto Sydney New Delhi

ATHENEUM BOOKS FOR YOUNG READERS • An imprint of Simon & Schuster Children's Publishing Division • 1230 Avenue of the Americas, New York, New York 10020 • Text copyright © 1969 by Judith Viorst • Text copyright renewed © 1997 by Judith Viorst • Illustrations copyright © 1969 by Arnold Lobel • Illustrations copyright renewed © 1997 by Adrianne Lobel and Adam S. Lobel • All rights reserved, including the right of reproduction in whole or in part in any form. • ATHENEUM BOOKS FOR YOUNG READERS is a registered trademark of Simon & Schuster, Inc. Atheneum logo is a trademark of Simon & Schuster, Inc. • For information about special discounts for bulk purchases, please contact Simon & Schuster Special Sales at 1-866-506-1949 or business@simonandschuster.com. • The Simon & Schuster Speakers Bureau can bring authors to your live event. For more information or to book an event, contact the Simon & Schuster Speakers Bureau at 1-866-248-3049 or visit our website at www.simonspeakers.com. • The text for this book was set in Helvetica Neue. • Manufactured in China • 0120 SCP • This Atheneum Books for Young Readers edition April 2020 . 10 9 8 7 6 5 4 3 2 1 • Library of Congress Cataloging-in-Publication Data • Names: Viorst, Judith, author. | Lobel, Arnold, illustrator. • Title: I'll fix Anthony / Judith Viorst ; illustrated by Arnold Lobel. • Other titles: I will fix Anthony • Description: First edition. | Originally published: New York : Harper & Row, 1969. | Audience: Ages 4–8. | Audience: Grades K–1. | Summary: A little brother thinks of the ways he will some day get revenge on his older brother. • Identifiers: LCCN 2019040928 | ISBN 9781534404816 (hardcover) | ISBN 9781534404830 (eBook) • Subjects: CYAC: Brothers—Fiction. | Sibling rivalry—Fiction. • Classification: LCC PZ7.V816 Il 2020 | DDC [E]—dc23 • LC record available at https://lccn.loc.gov/2019040928

To my mother and father, the ideal grandparents

My brother
Anthony

can read books now,

but he won't read any books to me.

He plays checkers
with Bruce
from his school.
But when
I want to play
he says, Go away or I'll clobber you.

I let him wear
my Snoopy sweat shirt,
but he never lets me
borrow his sword.

Mother says deep down
in his heart Anthony loves me.

Anthony says deep down
in his heart he thinks I stink.

Mother says deep deep down
in his heart,
where he doesn't even know it,
Anthony loves me.

YOU STINK

Anthony says
deep deep down
in his heart he still thinks I stink.

When I'm six

I'll fix Anthony.

When I'm six a dog

will follow me home,

and she'll beg for me and roll over
and lick my face.

If Anthony tries to pet her,
she'll give him a bite.

When I'm six Anthony will have
the German  measles,

and my father will take me
to a baseball game.

Then Anthony will have
the mumps,

and my mother will take me
to the flower show.

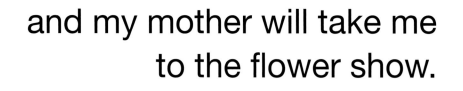

Then Anthony will have a virus,

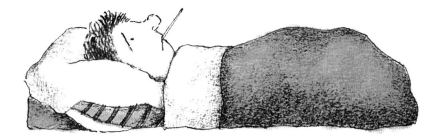

and my grandfather
will take me to the movies.

I won't have to save popcorn
for Anthony unless I want to.

When I'm six we'll have
a skipping contest,
and I'll skip faster.

Then we'll have
a jumping contest,
and I'll jump higher.

Then we'll
do Eeny-Meeny-Miney-Mo,
and Anthony
will be O-U-T.
He'll be very M-A-D.

When I'm six I'll read

Anthony will still
be reading

Who are you voting for, Anthony?
I'll ask him.

When I'm six I'll stand
on my head,
and my legs won't wobble.

Anthony's legs
will wobble a lot.

If someone tickles me,
I'll keep standing
on my head.

If someone pinches me,
I'll keep standing
on my head.

If someone says,
Give up
or I'll clobber you,
I'll keep standing on my head.
Anthony will give up at tickles.

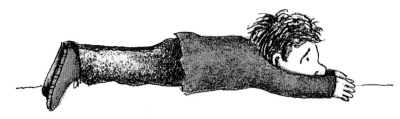

When I'm six I'll know how to

sharpen pencils.

Here's how you do it, Anthony, I'll say.

When I'm six I'll float,
but Anthony will sink
to the bottom.
I'll dive off the board,
but Anthony will change his mind.

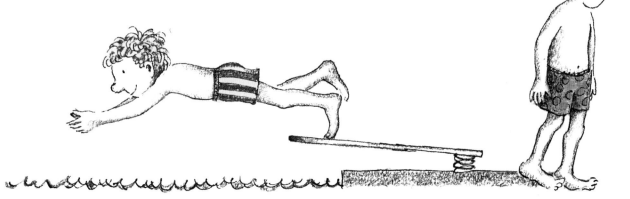

I'll breathe in and out when I should,
but Anthony will only go

GLUG GLUG

When I'm six I'll be tall, and Anthony will be short because I'll eat things like carrots and potatoes, and he'll eat things like jelly beans and root beer.

I'll put his red sneakers on the top shelf, and if he stands on a chair, he still won't be able to reach them.

He'll tell me,
Get down
my sneakers,
and I'll tell him,
Say please,

and if he doesn't say
please, he can't have
his sneakers
for a hundred
years.

When I'm six I'll add 7 and 4 and 10 and 3 inside my mind.

Anthony will just add 1 and 1 and 2, and he'll have to use his fingers.

When I'm six we'll have a race,
and I'll be at the corner when Anthony
hasn't even passed the fireplug.

The next time I'll give him
a head start, but it won't help.

When I'm six friends will call me on the telephone.

No one will call Anthony.

I'll sleep at Charlie's house and Eddie's and Diana's, but Anthony will always sleep at home.

See you later, Anthony, I'll tell him.

When I'm six
I'll help people
carry their groceries
from the supermarket,

and they'll say,
My, you're strong.

I don't think
Anthony
will be
strong enough.

When I'm six
I'll be able to tell
left and right,
but Anthony
will be all mixed up.

I'll be
able
to tell time,
but Anthony will be all mixed up.

I'll be able to tell my street and my city
and sometimes my zip code,
but Anthony will be all mixed up.

If he ever gets lost,
I guess I'll have to go find him.

When I'm six Anthony will still be falling off his bike.

I'll ride by with no hands.

Still falling off that bike? I'll ask Anthony.

When I'm six I'll let Dr. Ross
look down my throat
with a stick.

If he has to give me
a shot, I won't
even holler.

Try to be brave like your brother,
Dr. Ross will tell Anthony.

But Anthony
won't.

When I'm six  my teeth will fall out,

and I'll put them under the bed,
and the tooth fairy will take
them away and leave dimes.

Anthony's teeth
won't fall out.

He'll wiggle and wiggle them,
but they won't
fall out.

TEETH 25¢

I might sell him
one of my teeth,

but I might not.

When I'm six I'll go BINGO all the time.
Anthony won't even go BINGO once.

I'll win all the tic-tac-toes if I'm *X*,
and I'll win them all if I'm *O*.
Too bad, Anthony, I'll say.

Anthony is chasing me out
of the playroom.

He says I stink.
He says he is going to clobber me.
I have to run now, but I won't
have to run when I'm six.

When I'm six

I'll fix Anthony.